For all my family and friends in Maine.
Remember Fred!

Copyright © 2006 by Adria Meserve
All rights reserved
First published in Great Britain by The Bodley Head, an imprint of Random House Children's Books
Printed and bound in Singapore by Tien Wah Press
First American edition, 2006
1 3 5 7 9 10 8 6 4 2

www.fsgkidsbooks.com

Library of Congress Cataloging-in-Publication Data
Meserve, Adria.
    No room for Napoleon / Adria Meserve.— 1st American ed.
        p.   cm.
    Summary: When he arrives on a paradise island, Napoleon the dog
orders its friendly inhabitants to help him construct a big house that gradually
takes over all of the available space.
    ISBN-13: 978-0-374-35536-4
    ISBN-10: 0-374-35536-3
    [1. Dogs—Fiction.   2. Selfishness—Fiction.   3. Islands—Fiction.
4. Animals—Fiction.]   I. Title.

PZ7.M5484No 2006
[E]—dc22
                                                                    2005045073

No Room for Napoleon

Adria
Meserve

FARRAR STRAUS GIROUX
NEW YORK

Napoleon was a small brown dog with very **big ideas.**
One day, while he was out in his boat exploring,
he spotted land through his telescope.
"Perfect!" he said. **"My very own paradise island!"**

And he rowed ashore.

Napoleon strode up the beach.

Crab, Bunny, and Bear came out to greet him. "Welcome," they said. Crab gave Napoleon a beautiful pebble from the beach. Bunny hung a garland of flowers around his neck, and Bear invited him on a tour of the whole island.

Later, the
friends made
Napoleon a meal
fit for a king.

"Isn't this wonderful!" said Bear.
"**The best,**" said Napoleon. **"I'd like to stay."**
Crab, Bunny, and Bear were delighted.
"Let's make you a home!" they said.

Napoleon got very excited.
"I want it to be tall . . .

and wide . . .

with a great ocean view!"

Napoleon had so many ideas that he **scarfed down** his dinner as quick as he could and *rushed off* in search of . . .

just the right place!

"Why is he in such a hurry?" asked Crab.
"No idea," said Bunny.
"Never mind," said Bear. "Let's play!"

Early the next morning, Napoleon was already
busy building his new house.
Crab, Bunny, and Bear offered to help.

Napoleon gave his new
friends orders.

"Bear, bring me some branches!"

"Bunny, fetch some flowers!"

"Crab, pile up some pebbles!"

"He sounds very important,"
thought the three friends. So they
collected and stacked, while
Napoleon chopped and hammered.

As the friends did more and more, Napoleon did less and less. But . . .

he always kept an eye on them through his

telescope.

The one time Crab, Bunny,
and Bear stopped to play,
Napoleon barked,

"Jump to it! There is no time to waste!"

Napoleon made Crab, Bunny, and Bear work all through the day and all through the night.

Napoleon's
house grew

bigger . . .

and bigger . . .

. . . and bigger.

Crab, Bunny, and Bear's island got smaller and smaller, until
the woods, gardens, and beach had nearly disappeared.

At last Napoleon's
new house was
finished. He stood
at the top and
shouted,

"I'm the King of the Castle!"

"What is he talking about?" asked Crab. "No idea," said Bunny. "All I know is that he has used up everything on the island," said Bear, "and . . .

. . . there is no room left for us."

Crab, Bunny, and Bear
knew they had to
do something.

The next morning, King Napoleon
looked down from his castle.
"Where's my breakfast?" he said,
searching for his three friends . . .

. . . with his telescope.

No Crab . . .

No Bunny . . .

No Bear . . .

At last, Napoleon spotted them far out at sea.

King Napoleon strutted around
his kingdom. He dug holes,
he rolled in the dirt, he barked
and he howled, but no one
brought him his breakfast.

Napoleon looked for the three friends again.
They were on another island – having
A MEAL FIT FOR A KING.

"This isn't much fun!" he said.

His tummy rumbled.

Napoleon decided to row across to the other island to see his friends. But when he tried to row ashore, they said,

"No! There's no room for Napoleon!"

No one had ever said no to Napoleon before. "But why?" he asked.

"You used up all the pebbles and the trees and the flowers,"
said Crab.

"You wouldn't let us play,"
said Bunny.

"You spoiled our island,"
said Bear.

"You're a selfish dog!"
they all said.

Napoleon's ears drooped and his crown slid from
his head. He forgot all about being king.

"It's no fun on the island without you," he said.
"If I put everything back the way it was,
will you come home?"

"Maybe," said Crab.
   "I'm not sure," said Bunny.
      "You would have to make
         a lot of changes . . ." said Bear.

Napoleon got very excited.

"I'll knock the castle down!"

"I'll plant the most beautiful flowers!"

"I'll grow the tallest trees!"

Crab, Bunny, and Bear
were delighted. They helped
to collect seeds and plants to take back.
Then Napoleon climbed into
his boat and waved goodbye.
"You'll be able to come home soon!"
he promised.

Napoleon worked and worked and worked. When the friends finally came home, they couldn't believe their eyes! There were lush green trees and the most colorful flowers.

"This is even better than before!" the three friends said.
"Isn't our island beautiful!" said Bear.

"**THE BEST!**" said Napoleon.
"**If there's room, I'd love to stay!**"

"Of course you can!" the friends said.
"Now – let's **play**!"

But far out at sea . . .
a small ginger cat
spotted land through
her binoculars.
"Purrfect," she said.
*"My very own
paradise island . . ."*